Aurora
and the
Magical
Dance Shoes

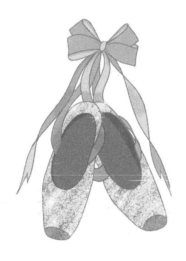

Written by Cecilia M. Pereyra

Illustrated by Jennifer Carroll

Madison + Park
A Global Branding Agency

I would like to dedicate this book to
those near and dear to my heart:

Aurora: Mommy, you are the definition of selflessness,
compassion, and strength. Thank you for being so loving and always
leading by example. You and Daddy have always been
extremely hard working and you inspire me to be resilient
and strive to make my dreams reality. I love you!

Brandon, Rosella, Nathaniel, and Raina: You are the air that
I breathe and my WHY every single day. Thank you for
being my beautiful blessings and purposes in life. Dream
big because the sky is the limit. I love you forever!

Francis: Thank you for your love and support always.
We were just two young kids who flourished and planted roots
to provide love, hope, and support for our children. I pray our
story inspires them. You are my everything! I love you!

Let me introduce you to a girl named Aurora who was shy, quiet, and bashful.

Her siblings were outgoing and friendly,

while she was **different**,
reserved and careful.

Aurora had a **secret** she kept to herself. She didn't share with her siblings or even a classmate.

Not even her mom, not even her dad, knew about this secret she kept that was
great.

Even though she was quiet

and embarrassed to talk in class,

She always dreamed of being a **dancer** who could twirl, leap, and prance.

One day, Aurora discovered a **secret trunk** locked away in a room of her house.

She was **curious** to find out what was inside.
Would it be a collection   of bags, hats, or
just a blouse?

She opened the trunk and inside was a letter
with a pair of golden sparkly shoes.

The letter said, "Wear these shoes for a **magical** dance, wherever your heart will choose."

Aurora put the magical dance shoes on and she
began to glow as she twirled

She danced up and down the walls of the room. She leaped out of the house and continued to dance around town.

and leaped around.

She twirled on top of bridges and

danced through the streets

She danced in the parks, pranced along the rivers to her own little beats.

This feeling inside was one

she couldn't forget—

Of happiness,

bliss, love,

and confidence!

The next morning, she was **excited** to share her dance tales and adventures

With her brother, sister,
parents, and those that she **treasures**.

She **shouted** out loud, I'm a dancer who can twirl, leap and prance!

With my magical dance shoes,
I can **fly, turn, and dance!**

She ran up to the room to find
her magical dance shoes
Only to find the room empty.
Aurora felt sad and confused.

There was **no trunk**, no letter, or magical dance shoes

She was **alone**, sad and full of the blues.

Aurora fell to the floor and was full of despair.

"How can I dance **without** my magical dance shoes?" she cried into the air.

When **suddenly**, Aurora heard a voice:
"Be happy and dance, go on and start!"
"You don't need magical shoes to dance,
Feel it in your **heart!**"

Aurora **looked up** to see her family around.

They
said,
"Go on Aurora,
you can do it!
Show us this
passion you
have found!"

Aurora
reached
deep down
inside to find
all her **courage**.

She closed her
eyes, took a deep
breath, and then
started to **flourish**.

Aurora **leaped** from side to side, began to twirl and prance.

She smiled all the way, saying,
"WOW, I really can dance!"

She realized she didn't
need the magical shoes
to dance.

It was inside of her the
whole time. She could
do it always at any
chance.

That day, Aurora's family said, "Never be scared and
always follow your dreams,
Be happy and be brave! Nothing is too large as it
seems!"

Being a dancer was a dream,

she never thought she could be

But, Aurora learned nothing was impossible

—just look inside yourself and see!

About the Author

Cecilia Pereyra has been dancing for as long as she can remember—from twirling around the house as a little girl to travelling the globe as a professional dancer. Today, she writes stories inspired by her four young children and her lifelong love of dance. As a Filipino-American, born in New Jersey and raised by parents from the Philippines, Cecilia is proud of her cultural upbringing and the value placed on family and faith. She lives in New Jersey with her husband, kids, and mother, Aurora. Cecilia hopes to encourage children of all ages to follow their passion and dream big.

About the Illustrator

Jennifer Carroll grew up in California but, proudly born in Manila, Philippines. Today, she is a full-time artist, wife, mother of two boys, and a local business owner of an all-women's gym in Charlotte, North Carolina. As an artist her entire life, creativity was an important outlet of expression. Among other creative talents such as costume and jewelry design, painting and illustration is her true passion. With an artistic approach and keen attention to detail, she weaves a story using various art techniques with various materials that bring to life expressive, memorable characters that move and define a picture.

CPSIA information can be obtained
at www.ICGtesting.com
Printed in the USA
LVHW071451220921
698454LV00002B/73